HORRIBLE HARRY
and the Dead Letters

Other Books by Suzy Kline

HORRIBLE HARRY
and the Dead Letters

BY **SUZY KLINE**
PICTURES BY **AMY WUMMER**

SCHOLASTIC INC.
New York Toronto London Auckland Sydney
Mexico City New Delhi Hong Kong Buenos Aires

ISBN-13: 978-0-545-19877-6
ISBN-10: 0-545-19877-1

Text copyright © 2008 by Suzy Kline.
Illustrations copyright © 2008 by Viking Children's Books.
All rights reserved. Published by Scholastic Inc.,
557 Broadway, New York, NY 10012, by arrangement with
Viking, a division of Penguin Young Readers Group, a member
of Penguin Group (USA) Inc. SCHOLASTIC and associated
logos are trademarks and/or registered trademarks of Scholastic Inc.

12 11 10 9 8 7 6 5 4 3 2 1   9 10 11 12 13 14/0

Printed in the U.S.A.   40

First Scholastic printing, October 2009

Set in New Century Schoolbook
Illustrations by Amy Wummer

Special appreciation to . . .

Joyce Cullum, a dedicated librarian at Byron Bergen Elementary in Bergen, New York, for her creative mailbox activities!

Eileen Spinelli and her wonderful book *If You Want to Find Golden*.

My editor, Catherine Frank, for her hard work and enthusiasm.

And to my husband, Rufus, who read the first drafts. I love you!

Contents

CONTENTS

A Letter from Doug

Dear Reader,

My friend Harry has been a detective now for over a year. He solved his first case, The Case of the Missing Pixie Dust, on Halloween in second grade. When Harry got to third grade, he took on three big mysteries:

The Case of the Locked Closet
The Case of the Groom in Room 3B
The Case of the Orange-Sticker Winners

Harry solved two of them and botched one. All together that's three out of four. In baseball, Harry would be batting cleanup, fourth in the lineup with a .750 average. That's pretty good!

When Harry is not on a case, he likes fooling around with horrible things. Usually, they make good stories, and I write about them:

Spiders, ants, and earwigs
Snakes and lizards
Tasmanian devils and fire-eating
   dragons!
Stinkhorn mushrooms and green
   slime

I never thought horrible things

could help Harry solve a mystery, but they sure did this time! And it was a new kind of horrible too.

Harry's horrible poems! They actually helped us crack The Case of the Dead Letters.

Do you wonder how Harry got interested in poetry? And what these dead letters are all about?

I'll explain everything! It's all connected, and it started with a rainbow. Just read on!

Your friend,

Doug

A Rainbow in Room 3B

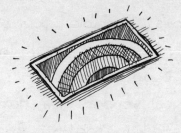

It was Monday morning. We were just hanging up our jackets in Room 3B, and we looked like a rainbow! It was "Wear Your Favorite Color Day" in Miss Mackle's third-grade class. Song Lee and ZuZu were dressed in red. Ida was wearing purple. Dexter was in blue. I had a green shirt on with matching green socks. Harry was dressed in brown. Mary and Sidney were both wearing pink.

"Don't you know pink is for girls?" Mary said.

Sid put his nose right next to Mary's. "For your information, Mare, my step-dad has the exact same pink shirt. It's high fashion."

Mary rolled her eyes. "Maybe on planet Mars!" she groaned. When a couple of kids giggled, Sid made a face.

"You don't know everything!" Sid snapped.

"No," Mary replied. "But I do know my colors, King Pinky Toes!"

"No you don't, Queen Hairy Toes!" Sid shot back.

I tried not to laugh.

That morning Miss Mackle sat down in her big teacher chair in front of the room.

"Your rainbow earrings are pretty," Ida said.

The teacher smiled and said thank you.

"Now, boys and girls," she said, "I want to read you some poems about colors. They're from the book *If You Want to Find Golden* by Eileen Spinelli."

Harry made a face. "Ugh," he groaned. Then he sank down in his chair and closed his eyes. Harry did not like poetry.

Everyone else listened politely to the poems about red fire engines, an orange marmalade cat, a pesky yellow bee, and gray chimney smoke. When

Miss Mackle read the one about brown roasted peanuts, Harry opened his eyes and started sniffing. I think he smelled them!

And when she finished reading the last poem, about silver tinkling party sounds, Harry put two thumbs up.

Miss Mackle beamed. "Now, I have a treat for each one of you." And she held something up. "It's a sparkly rainbow bookmark with a list of one hundred and twenty colors on the back!"

It was so cool!

"Thank you!" we all said as she passed them out.

"Way cool!" Harry added. "I didn't know there were so many names for brown!"

I looked at the list. I didn't either!

auburn
copper
taupe
brown
mahogany
khaki
buff
ochre
ecru
burnt sienna
rust
beige
burnt umber

sepia
bronze

"Ohhh," Mary exclaimed. "The list includes my favorite color of light green—celadon!"

"How about fourteen names for pink!" Sid exclaimed, waving both hands in the air.

pink
shocking pink
carnation

tea rose
fuchsia
rose
magenta
deep pink
cerise
Japanese pink
hot pink
French rose
cherry blossom
puce

"I suppose you're wearing hot pink tomorrow, Sid," Mary teased.

"Actually, I'm wearing magenta," Sidney replied.

"Okay," the teacher exclaimed. "Now it's your turn to write your own color poetry."

Our Color Poems

"First," the teacher said, "choose any color. Then start and end with this phrase." Miss Mackle walked over to the blackboard and wrote in cursive: *If you want to find . . .*

"And remember," the teacher continued, "to begin the other lines in your poem with an action word. And mention a few of your senses."

Harry got right to work on his brown poem.

I got right to work too. The first sentence was easy. *If you want to find blue!*
After I wrote eight lines in my notebook, I read them to myself:

If you want to find blue,
jump into a lake!
Eat a blueberry pie then
look in the mirror
at your BLUE TEETH!
Lie down on the grass and
look up at the summer sky
if you want to find blue.

I leaned back in my chair feeling like a poet!

Fifteen minutes later, Miss Mackle asked, "Is anyone ready to read their color poem?"

Harry waved his hand in the air. "I am!"

"Good! Go ahead, Harry," the teacher said.

Harry stood up tall, and started reading:

"If you want to find brown,
go barefoot on a farm.
Step on a fresh cow patty and
wiggle your toes!
Feel the cow doo-doo
cool off your piggies
if you want to find brown."

Lots of us laughed.

Sidney and Harry slapped each other five.

Miss Mackle wagged her finger. "I wouldn't want any of you to step on cow manure. You might get germs! I suggest, Harry, you think of something else to step on that is brown."

"Yeah! Not cow poop!" Mary snapped. "That's disgusting!"

"I'll work on it," he replied.

Sid went next.

"If you want to find pink,
look at my pink crayon.
Wear a pink shirt like me,
take a ride in a pink car,
and toot the horn!
Or eat some strawberry ice cream
if you want to find pink."

Miss Mackle smiled. "I love the strawberry ice cream part!"

Everyone clapped except Mary.

ZuZu made a comment. "Crayons aren't always pink, though, Sid, and neither are shirts and cars."

"How about pinkeye, then," Sid replied, darting back to his seat. When he got there, he added something else. "And cotton candy! I'm inspired now!"

When Mary twirled her finger in the air, pretending to be excited, Sidney looked hurt.

Later that morning when we were finishing up our writing, Miss Mackle announced, "I have a big surprise for you, class!"

The Big Surprise

Miss Mackle stepped out into the hallway. We could hear our custodian, Mr. Beausoleil, talking.

"Be careful now," he said. "It's heavy."

They both carried something big and blue into Room 3B.

"*A mailbox!*" we all exclaimed.

"The post office said this was an old one and that it could be used for

educational purposes," Miss Mackle explained.

We watched the teacher pull down the blue handle and show us the mail chute. It worked!

"So, what do you think, class? Do you want a genuine mailbox in Room 3B?"

"*Yes!*" we all shouted.

"Thanks, Mr. Beausoleil," the teacher said as the custodian waved and walked out the door.

Miss Mackle turned to our monitors chart. "We have post-office jobs now," she said, tacking a new sign to the bulletin board. "We'll rotate them each week so everyone will have a turn to be postmaster."

Postmaster—Mary
Facer—Harry

Nixer—ZuZu
Canceller—Song Lee
Sorter—Ida
Carriers—Doug, Dexter, Sid

"What does the postmaster do?" Mary asked.

"The postmaster is like the captain of a team," Miss Mackle explained. "You make sure the post office runs smoothly. You can call a meeting, and you are in charge of this key."

The teacher held up a string necklace with a metal key.

Mary's eyes doubled in size!

"Every day after lunch recess, you will use this key to unlock the mailbox. Once the door is open, you'll scoop the letters into this crate. Then you'll carry the crate to your supply table for

19

sorting. When you're not using the key, hang it up on the hook next to the monitor's chart."

"I love it, Miss Mackle!" Mary tried on the key necklace right away.

"What's a facer?" Harry asked.

"A facer makes sure the letters are stacked so the address is on top," Miss Mackle replied.

Harry nodded. "That's easy. What's the canceller?"

"The canceller postmarks all the letters with a rubber stamp."

Song Lee squeezed her hands together and smiled. "I'm the canceller. I get to do that! Do I have a stamp, Miss Mackle?"

"You sure do. It's a special rainbow stamp."

"Ohhh!" Song Lee said, clapping her hands.

"Now, I want the post-office staff to come over with me to the supply table," the teacher said.

Eight of us joined her.

She pointed out the plastic milk-carton crate, one shoe box, a stack of paper, envelopes, a stamp pad and stamp, stickers, pencils, pens, and markers.

I noticed Sidney take one envelope

and return to his desk for a minute.

"I'm the nixer," ZuZu said. "What's that?"

"Nixer comes from the word, *nix*, which means *no*," Miss Mackle explained. "A nixie is a letter that is not addressed properly. So, if a letter has no address or name, the nixer puts it in the Dead Letter Office." Miss Mackle held up the shoe box.

"That shoe box is an office?" ZuZu asked.

Miss Mackle chuckled. "You'll have to use your imagination."

"And maybe a pen," ZuZu said, taking a black marker from the supply table. We all watched him neatly write two words on top of the shoe box:

DEAD LETTERS

"Dum de dum dum," Harry sang out.

Everyone giggled, even Mary.

"I get to deliver the mail," Dexter said.

"Me too!" I said, slapping him five.

Sidney tiptoed over to the mailbox and dropped in his envelope.

"We're not starting to mail things yet, Sidney!" Miss Mackle called out.

Sid jumped a mile! I think he was quite surprised the teacher saw him.

"S-sorry!" Sid stammered.

"How do I sort the letters?" Ida asked.

"By rows," the teacher answered. "So everyone be sure to write the row number below the person's name on the envelope."

"Did you do that, Sidney?" Mary asked.

Sidney shook his head.

Mary used her key to open up the door at the bottom half of the big blue mailbox. She took out the one white envelope and carried it over to ZuZu.

"If it has no address, it goes into the Dead Letter Office," Mary said.

"It doesn't have a name either," ZuZu added as he dropped Sid's letter into the shoe box, then attached the lid and two rubber bands.

Sid didn't seem to care very much. He just shrugged. "I only wrote one sentence."

Miss Mackle smiled. "Well, I think we should give Sidney a second chance. I don't think he heard my directions."

Just as ZuZu started to undo the two rubber bands, Sidney objected. "No, no! I want my goof to remind people to address their mail correctly. Just leave it there as a dead letter."

"Well," the teacher replied, "I think we should give Sidney a round of applause for helping us to remember an important rule. I just hope we only have one dead letter!"

Sidney grinned after everyone clapped.

When we returned to our seats, Mary went bonkers!

The Mystery Begins!

"**M**y rainbow bookmark is gone!" Mary exclaimed. "And it was my favorite one ever!"

"Oh, I'm sure it will turn up," Miss Mackle said. "I know how aggravating it is to misplace something."

"But I didn't misplace it. I had it right on top of my desk!" Mary barked. "Someone just swiped it!"

I looked under my desk. So did Harry. I was wondering if he might consider it a possible case. But it looked doubtful. Kids on our class were always losing stuff.

"Somebody probably picked it up accidentally," Ida said. "The bookmarks all look alike. It's easy to do."

"Boys and girls, please check to see if you have two bookmarks," Miss Mackle said.

Everyone looked in their desk.

No one had two.

Miss Mackle squatted down next to Mary. They were eye to eye now. "If I

had an extra one, I would give it to you. I'm sure your bookmark will turn up, Mary."

They both nodded.

Then the teacher held up her big glass jar. It had nineteen pieces of folded paper inside, and each paper had a student's name written on it. "Each day I will ask you to pick one name out of this jar. You will write to that person. The next day we'll draw again."

"What if we get the same person?" ZuZu asked. "Or ourselves?"

"Just refold the paper and put it back into the jar and draw again," the teacher said.

"Let's get down to biz!" Harry said, rubbing his hands together. "I want to write a poem for someone!"

We picked names from the glass jar

and started writing. I got lucky! I got ZuZu's name. I decided to send him my blue poem.

After lunch, we took care of our post-office chores. Mary opened the mail-box with her metal key. When Harry leaned over her shoulder to watch, she nudged him away. "I need room. *Excuuuuuse* me!" Mary said with lots of expression.

She scooped all the letters into the milk carton crate and carried it over to the post office table. After she dumped it, Harry quickly stacked the letters so the names and row numbers were faceup. ZuZu flipped through the pile and looked for errors. "No dead letters today!" he said.

Song Lee stamped each one care-fully with a rainbow stamp. Not one rainbow was upside down. Then Ida sorted them by rows. Dexter, Sid, and I each picked up a pile of letters and began our routes. Dexter hummed an Elvis tune as he delivered the letters to his row. It didn't take long. Soon, everyone had mail and began opening it up.

Some kids sent pictures. Some sent their poems like Harry and I did. ZuZu did a crossword puzzle for Harry. He loved it.

"What's a four-letter word for 'get lost'?" Harry asked.

"*Scat!*" Mary said. "Dexter sent me a dot-to-dot. I think it's a house. But I'm not sure."

"It's Elvis's Heartbreak Hotel," Dexter replied, and then he sang the song for her.

For the next two days, we continued writing letters and different kinds of poetry. Song Lee liked writing haiku. Harry loved writing odes. Those were poems with lots of feeling. He showed me the one he wrote to leeches:

Oh, leeches!
You crazy bloodsucking worms.
I know you have

thirty-four segments and
two suckers!
I remember that day I fell in the
    pond—
you jumped on
my arms and legs and
sucked my blood.
Song Lee saved me with
her soy sauce.
Oh, leeches!
Why don't you drink ketchup?

"What do you think?" Harry asked.

"I think your ode is . . . different,"
I said. Actually, it gave me goose pim-
ples. But I left that part out.

The next day something very weird
happened.

Something Weird

Thursday morning, after everyone drew a piece of paper from the glass jar and got busy writing, Ida stood up and looked around. "Has anyone seen my rainbow bookmark? It isn't in my desk!"

"I don't see my bookmark either!" Song Lee replied. "I put it inside my Henry Huggins book. It was on page forty-five."

"Wait a minute," Sid said. "My book-mark is gone too!"

Miss Mackle stopped helping a student. "What is going on? If anyone knows anything about this, please speak up now."

The class turned pin quiet.

Miss Mackle asked everyone to check their backpacks. "Maybe some-one accidentally picked up a bookmark and thought it was theirs. If you have two, then that would help solve our problem."

Everyone emptied their book bags.

No luck!

"Let's empty all our desks and clean them out," Miss Mackle ordered.

Sidney grabbed his desk with both hands and tipped it forward. Everything dumped out: books, pens, pencils, wads

of paper, two used Kleenexes, an old black banana, and some hairy-monster-head erasers.

No one found an extra bookmark.

"They can't just vanish into thin air," Harry said. "Four missing bookmarks? That's a real mystery. It's a case I want to solve!"

"Good!" Mary grumbled. "I haven't had a bookmark for almost four days now, and no one's done anything about it. It's not fair!"

Harry turned around and shot me a

look. "Doug, will you help me with my investigation?"

"I sure will!" I answered, holding two thumbs up.

At lunch recess, Harry and I met by the Dumpster. We could talk there. It was private. "So who do you think is taking the bookmarks?" I asked.

Harry didn't answer. He pulled two baseball caps out of his back pockets

and put them on. One brim faced forward and one faced back. "I have to look like Sherlock Holmes to solve this humdinger of a case!" Harry said.

"Right," I agreed. I thought his deerslayer hat looked neat.

"I know one thing," Harry said. "Our thief is as sneaky as a leech."

Suddenly Harry's eyes bulged.

"What's the matter?" I asked.

"My leech ode to Song Lee!" Harry exclaimed. "I was in such a hurry to mail my letter, I can't remember if I put Song Lee's name or address on the envelope!"

"Oh, boy!" I said.

"I have to go in," Harry said.

"In where?" I replied.

"The classroom," Harry replied. "I've

got to open up the mailbox and check on my letter. If I don't, it could end up in the Dead Letter Office. I can't have that happen to my best poem!"

I rolled my eyes. I kind of liked the idea of Harry's leech ode ending up in the Dead Letter Office, but I wasn't going to tell him that.

"You'll get in big trouble if you sneak into the classroom now!" I warned.

Harry snapped his fingers. "You're right! So let's go play some kickball!"

"Huh?" I was totally confused. It was like Harry had tossed the whole idea of being a detective on a big case right out the window!

But I couldn't have been more wrong! It was all part of Harry's plan.

Harry's Kickball Plan

"*Play ball!*" Harry shouted as he pitched to ZuZu.

"Fast and over the plate, please," ZuZu said, rolling the red rubber ball back. Harry pitched again. ZuZu ran up and kicked it hard into center field.

Song Lee was there to make the catch.

"Way to go!" Harry yelled. As soon as we got two more people out, our team was up.

Harry weaseled his way to the head of the line. "I kick first," he called out.

ZuZu pitched him a fastball over the plate.

"Kick it to the moon!" Mary said.

"This baby is going to another planet!" Harry promised.

Everyone watched.

Harry ran up and kicked the ball hard. It didn't go into center field, left field, or right field. It careened into foul territory over the fence! Smack dab into the vacant lot where the mushrooms grow under the oak tree.

"Oh, no . . . !" everyone groaned.

"Now we can't play," Mary whined. "The game's over! We don't have a ball. Good going, Harry!"

Harry held up a finger. "It's no biggie—I'll take care of it. Yo, Doug,

come with me." And I raced over with him to Miss Mackle. She was walking around the playground supervising.

"Miss Mackle," Harry said, half out of breath. "May Doug and I go get another ball from the classroom? I just kicked ours over the fence. I'm so sorry!"

Miss Mackle looked at her watch. "We do have fifteen more minutes of recess, so go ahead, boys. Be quick!"

"Like lightning!" Harry promised.

Having permission to go back to the classroom was great! But how many minutes did Harry have to get the key, open the mailbox, find his letter, and possibly address it to Song Lee?

Three? Four? I looked at my watch. It said 12:30 P.M. Five minutes would look suspicious.

"Lightning quick, Harry," I repeated. This caper had to be *fast!*

We walked quickly up the stairs to the second-floor hallway. When we didn't see a teacher, we made a mad dash for Room 3B.

Harry ducked inside and got the string necklace off the hook. I made a beeline for the supply closet and got another red rubber ball.

Harry had no trouble unlocking the

bottom of the mailbox. As soon as he pulled the door down, he reached inside and scooped out all the letters.

"Whoa, look at this, Doug!" Harry exclaimed. "I found a treasure."

I rushed over to him.

There it was at the bottom of the mailbox.

"Three rainbow bookmarks!" The

Postmaster	Mary
Facer	Harry
Nixer	ZuZu
Canceller	Song Lee
Sorter	Ida
Carriers	Doug Dexter Sid

red rubber ball fell out of my hands.

"Cool hiding place, huh?" Harry said. "No wonder no one found them."

I grabbed the ball and held it tight. "Anyone could have dropped those bookmarks in the mailbox. I just wonder who."

"Me too," Harry agreed.

"What . . . what are you going to do with them?" I asked, checking my watch.

Harry slowly shook his head. "Nothing. I'm going to leave them right where they are. I'll let Mary find them when she opens the mailbox after recess. It will be one big happy celebration. I'll bet the thief got cold feet and wanted to return the bookmarks the same day."

I looked at my watch again. "Harry,

it's been almost four minutes. If we don't leave now, we're doomed."

"You're right, Doug. Help me put these letters back into the mailbox."

I did. Harry slammed the door shut and hung up the key, and we took off!

As soon as the kids saw us running out of the building with the rubber ball, they all cheered.

I was relieved. We made it!

"So did you remember to put Song Lee's address on her letter?" I asked.

Harry slowed down and bopped himself on the head with the ball. "Man! I can't believe it. I completely forgot!"

"I guess you're more of a detective than a poet," I said.

"Yeah," Harry moaned. "I'll find out soon enough about Song Lee's letter."

"Play ball!" we both shouted.

The Mailbox Treasure

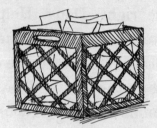

When we got back to the room after recess, it was post-office time. Harry and I couldn't wait to hear everyone cheer when they saw the treasure. Mary was going to jump into the air!

We stood next to her while she was unlocking the mailbox.

"I need room, you guys!" she scolded. "You're too close." And she elbowed us back a few steps.

Harry and I tried to look over her shoulder, but it was hard.

Mary scooped the letters into the plastic crate, closed the door, and relocked it.

She was not jumping into the air!

Harry and I stared at the mail. The three rainbow bookmarks weren't in the crate!

"Are you sure you got everything?" Harry asked.

"Of course I'm sure!" Mary replied, hanging up her key. "Okay, guys! It's time to do our post-office chores."

Everyone followed Mary to the supply table except Harry and me. We didn't move. We just froze.

"I can't believe it!" I whispered.

"I can," Harry whispered back. "Mary

is our thief! She is the one who hid those bookmarks in the mailbox. And she's keeping them there for another day!"

"But why?" I asked. "What could Mary be thinking?"

"I know what she's thinking!" Harry exclaimed. *"If I can't have a bookmark, no one else can either!"*

I chuckled. "Yeah, that sounds like Mary."

"So what do we do now?" I asked.

"Wait," Harry replied. "This case is not quite solved. We still need to find that fourth bookmark."

"Man, I forgot about that!" And then I rolled my eyes. This case had too many curveballs for me!

Harry and I joined the post-office table.

"I already faced the mail," Mary snapped. "You were late getting here, Harry."

"Sorry!" Harry said. "I was taking care of old business."

ZuZu was nixing the mail. "Hey, this one has no name or address. It's too bad." And he put it in the Dead Letter Office.

"Dum de dum dum!" Mary hummed. "That makes two dead letters!"

A couple of kids giggled. But Harry didn't.

His eyes bulged. He had forgotten to address Song Lee's letter. Now his best poem, his "Ode to Leeches," was in the Dead Letter Office.

We both took a couple of steps back.

"I have to get it," Harry whispered to me. "Can you take your time on that

mail delivery, Doug-o? I just need a few more minutes. Stall the mailmen!"

After Song Lee stamped the last letter, she got a long face. I knew why. She thought she wasn't getting any mail today.

Ida sorted the letters carefully into piles. Sid, Dexter, and I each picked up a bundle.

"Hey, Sid and Dex!" I called.

"Yeah?" they answered.

"Why don't we all sing an Elvis tune while we deliver the mail today. That would be cool."

"But I don't know the lyrics," Sid said.

"I can teach you one verse real easy," Dexter said.

Perfect, I thought. It would buy

three more minutes. While Dexter was going over one verse, Sid and I listened attentively.

Mary came over to see what we were doing. "Why aren't you passing out the mail?" she asked.

Harry seized the moment. Mary was away from the post-office table, and so was everyone else. I could see Harry reach for the Dead Letter box. He quickly removed the two rubber bands. One flew off into the air, but Harry just let it go. After he took the lid off, he paused for a moment. There were two envelopes in his hand. I knew what he was thinking: *Which one?*

Suddenly Harry dropped them both, bent over, and stuffed them in his shirt.

I knew it was part of his plan.

Harry then grabbed a new envelope, licked it, and popped it inside the Dead Letter Office. Phew!

He put that one rubber band on just in time. Mary was marching back to the table.

"What a mess!" Mary exclaimed. "I'm calling a meeting about the neatness of our supply table. Our Dead Letter Office is even missing a rubber band!"

"Good idea!" Harry said. Then he gave me the A-OK sign.

"Time to deliver the mail," I announced to Sid and Dexter. "We can sing that first verse now."

And that's when we started singing about blue, blue, blue suede shoes!

The Dead Letters

After we made our singing delivery, Harry motioned for me to meet him in the library corner.

He had the two dead letters in his hand. One was the letter to Song Lee. The other had something in it. A letter with one sentence and . . .

"The fourth bookmark!" I said. Quickly I covered my mouth.

"It was in the Dead Letter Office all the time," Harry added.

"All right!" I said. "Mystery solved!"

"Yup," Harry agreed. "I think it's going to be a very interesting post-office meeting."

"We're having one?" I asked.

"Mary's calling one. Perfect, huh?" Harry said as he addressed Song Lee's letter and handed it to me.

"Okey-dokey!" I said. "Time for me to deliver Song Lee's mail." And I raced over to her desk.

"Oh, thank you, Doug!" Song Lee exclaimed. "I was thinking I wasn't going to get any mail today."

"This letter may have gotten dropped. It never got stamped," I said. I was glad half of what I said was true.

Harry popped up behind me and looked over Song Lee's shoulder. "This is a good day," he said. "Hope you enjoy my 'Ode to Leeches.'"

Song Lee smiled back. "I know I will! I love your odes, Harry. They make me laugh."

Just as Harry flashed Song Lee a toothy grin, Mary made her big announcement.

"Attention, everyone on the post-office staff, please meet me at the supply table. We're having an important meeting."

Harry and I tried not to smile as we sat down at the long table. There were eight of us. Miss Mackle was reading poetry with a small group in the library corner.

"What's so important we have to have a meeting?" Sid asked.

Mary stood up. "My staff is not working neatly enough. Just look at the mess on our supply table. And my staff needs to be more prompt. Harry, you were so late today, I had to do your chore. And the mail delivery was delayed three minutes!"

Dexter and Sid shrugged.

Harry raised his hand. "Speaking of delivery, I think it's time to deliver this." And he handed Sidney a letter that had no address. "I thought you might want this back from the Dead Letter Office."

Sidney looked like he had just seen a ghost.

"Take it, Sid," Harry said, handing it to him.

Mary blew her bangs in the air. "Who said you could take that letter out of the Dead Letter Office, Harry Spooger?"

ZuZu lowered his eyebrows. "That mail is supposed to stay in the shoe box."

"Tell Mary who the dead letter is supposed to be to, Sid," Harry ordered.

Sid spoke so softly no one could hear him.

"Louder, Sid," Harry insisted.

"To Mary."

"Me?" Mary put out her hand. She didn't object anymore. "Give it to me!"

Sid handed it to her.

Mary looked inside the envelope. *"My rainbow bookmark!"*

Sid stood up. "I wrote one sentence in the letter."

Mary read it aloud. "'Here is your bookmark, Mary.'"

"I tried to mail it to you secretly," Sid said, "and get it back to you right away. You were bugging me about wearing pink and making fun of my poem. I wanted to get even. I never meant to keep the bookmark for very long. But when it landed in the Dead Letter Office, I was stuck. Everyone would know I was the one who took it." Sidney kept wiping his eyes. I could tell he felt bad. "I was going to give you my bookmark, but it got lost."

"You should have told me, Sidney LaFleur. It would have saved us all the aggravation!"

"Speaking of aggravation," Harry replied, "what about Sid's and Ida's and Song Lee's bookmarks? Hmmm, Mary?"

Mary's eyes started to water. "I knew you were spying on me today, Harry, when I opened up the mailbox."

Harry shrugged. He wasn't going to tell Mary how he really found out.

Mary got up and walked over to the mailbox. She opened up the bottom door with her key and got out the three bookmarks. When she returned to the table, she gave each one back.

"Why did you take mine?" Song Lee asked.

"And why did you take mine?" Ida asked.

Mary started to cry. "I am so sorry!

No one was doing anything about my bookmark. It wasn't fair. I didn't have one! I guess I thought I'd feel better if my friends and Sidney didn't have one either."

Harry and I nodded. We got the motive right.

"Misery loves company," ZuZu said. "My dad told me about that old saying. I guess it's true."

Ida and Song Lee were quiet for a moment.

"I am so sorry," Mary said. "I made a terrible decision. I was going to return them to you tomorrow, on Friday."

Song Lee came over and gave Mary a hug.

Ida did too.

"I don't deserve friends like you," Mary said, hugging them back.

"We know you feel bad," Song Lee said. "You're sorry, and you told us the truth."

"We forgive you," Ida replied. "You returned our bookmarks."

Harry and I slapped each other ten. "We solved our fifth case, Doug!" Harry said.

"We sure did!"

Everyone had their bookmarks and that makes for a happy ending to my story. But it wasn't a happy ending for

Mary and Sidney. When our teacher found out what was going on, those two lost their post-office jobs, and recess for two days. The worst part was that Miss Mackle called their parents, and they had to do a poetry project together. The teacher said they needed to be nicer to each other. She also said boys and girls can wear any color. Including pink.

"Hey, Doug!" Harry said as we were putting on our jackets to go home. "I celebrated our great detective work by writing another ode. And this time it's for you."

"Really? Thanks, man," I said, putting down my backpack.

Harry read it to me.

"Oh, mailbox!
You have so many surprises!
Some are good,
some are bad,
some make me happy,
and some make me sad.
Oh, mailbox!
Keep flipping your lid!

"So what do you think, Doug?"
"I think you're a better detective
than a poet!"
Harry just laughed.

Color Poems by Room 3B

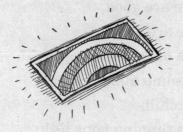

If You Want to Find Red
by Song Lee Park

If you want to find red,
look for a ladybug
or a cardinal flying by.
Peel off the Band-Aid on your knee
and smell the blood.
Taste a strawberry or
some watermelon
if you want to find red.

If You Want to Find Yellow
by Mary Berg

If you want to find yellow,
smell a lovely buttercup
or a juicy lemon.
Listen to the canary go *chirp, chirp.*
Watch a school bus go down the
    street or
feel the warm rays of the sun
if you want to find yellow.

If You Want to Find Pink
(revised)
by Sidney La Fleur

If you want to find pink,
eat some strawberry ice cream
or cotton candy at the fair.
Look at someone's pinkeye

or the inside of a wiener
if you want to find pink.

If You Want to Find Purple
by Ida Burrell

If you want to find purple,
look at the bruise on your leg.
Eat an eggplant or a Bermuda onion,
look at some purple majesties
    (mountains),
or play with Barney
if you want to find purple.

If You Want to Find Green
by ZuZu Hadad

If you want to find green,

look at an inchworm hanging from
    a tree.
Drink limeade or
eat key lime pie.
Listen to a parrot squawk, "Polly
    want a cracker,"
or watch the Oakland A's play base-
    ball on TV
if you want to find green.

If You Want to Find Blue
by Dexter Sanchez

If you want to find blue,
look at Elvis's blue suede shoes.
When you're sad,
you feel blue,
like Elvis when he sang the
    words,

"Christmas Without You."
Sing "Christmas Without You"
if you want to find blue.

If You Want to Find Celadon
by Mary Berg (first stanza) and
Sidney La Fleur (second stanza)

If you want to find celadon,
bite into some celery or
crunch on some lettuce.
Go to a museum and look at a celadon
    vase
if you want to find celadon.

If you want to find celadon,
look at a green tree python
or blow your nose when you have a
    cold,

then look what's inside your Kleenex,
if you want to find celadon.

If You Want to Find Brown
(revised)
by Harry Spooger

If you want to find brown,
go barefoot on a farm after it rains.
Step in the mud and
wiggle your toes!
Feel the muck
ooze between your piggies and moo
　　twice.
If you want to find brown.